Margaret K. McElderry Books
Macmillan Publishing Company
866 Third Avenue
New York, NY 10022

Maxwell Macmillan Canada, Inc.
1200 Eglinton Avenue East
Suite 200
Don Mills, Ontario M3C 3N1

Macmillan Publishing Company is part of the Maxwell Communication
Group of Companies.
First United States edition
A Vanessa Hamilton Book
Designed by Mark Foster
First published 1994 by Hamish Hamilton Ltd., London
Printed and bound in China by Imago
10 9 8 7 6 5 4 3 2 1
The illustrations are rendered in acrylic.
Library of Congress Catalog Card Number: 93-80959
ISBN 0-689-50616-3

MARGARET MAHY
The Christmas Tree Tangle

Illustrated by
ANTHONY KERINS

MARGARET K. McELDERRY BOOKS
New York
Maxwell Macmillan Canada
Toronto
Maxwell Macmillan International
New York   Oxford   Singapore   Sydney

Goodness gracious, what do I see?
The kitten has climbed the Christmas tree!
Climbed so high and climbed so far
To cling with her claws to the Christmas star.
Far, far above the town,
She mews and mews, but can't come down.
Everyone hears her caterwaul:
Help! Help! – or the kitten will fall.

Goodness gracious, what do I see?
The cat is climbing the Christmas tree.
Watch her scrabbling, watch her scratch –
The black-and-white cat with the ginger patch.
She follows the kitten who climbed so far
To cling with her claws to the Christmas star.
The cat will rescue the kitten now.

But, horrakapotchkin! What do I see?
She's tangled her tail and can't pull free.
Oh, what terrible Christmas luck:
Help! Help! – for the cat is stuck.

Goodness gracious, what do I see?
The dog is climbing the Christmas tree.
Past the cat with the tangled tail –
Who twists and tugs and begins to wail –
To free the kitten who climbed so far
To cling with her claws to the Christmas star.
Branch to branch, and bough to bough,
The dog will rescue the kitten now.

But nobody told him dogs can't climb.
He's having a terribly tumbly time.
Beware, below there! Mercy me!
Now, the dog is trapped in the tree.
His nose is dry and his ears go flop.
Help! Help! – or the dog will drop.

Goodness gracious, what do I see?
The goat is climbing the Christmas tree.
With lily-white beard and cheerful bleat,
She bobs and bounds on high-heeled feet
Past the cat with the tangled tail –
Who splits the night with a woeful wail –
And past the dog who barks with fright
(Bow-wow-wow! in the Christmas night),
To save the kitten who climbed so far
To cling with her claws to the Christmas star.

Branch to branch, and bough to bough,
The goat will rescue the kitten now.
But branches baffle her high-heeled feet,
And so the goat begins to bleat.
She slips and slides. She starts to sprawl.
Help! Help! – or the goat will fall.

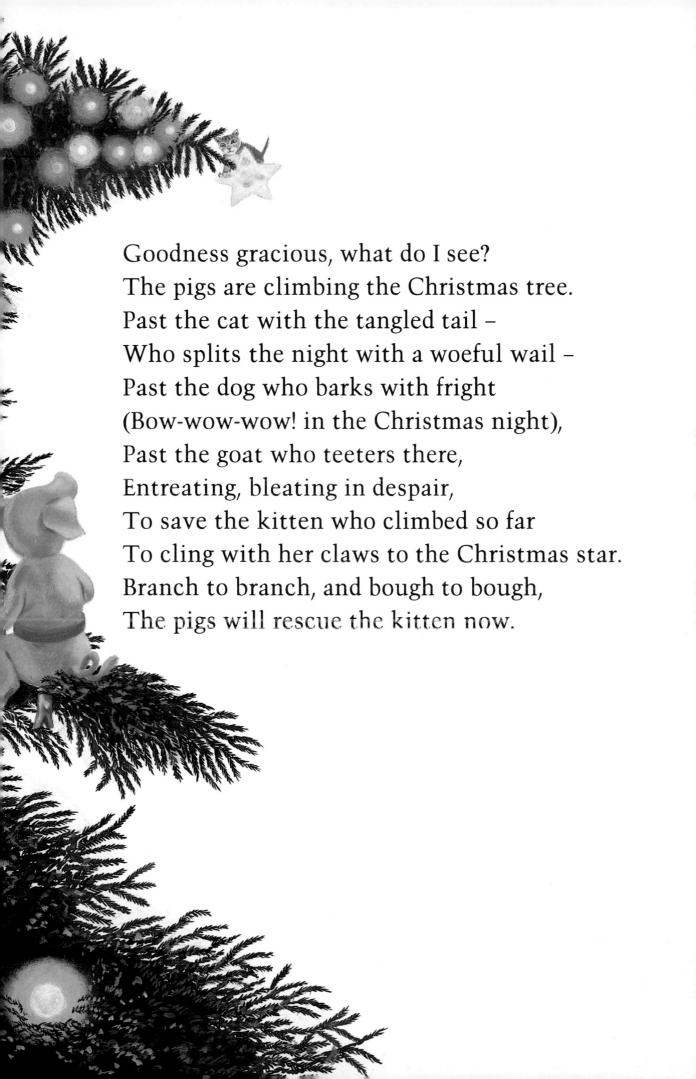

Goodness gracious, what do I see?
The pigs are climbing the Christmas tree.
Past the cat with the tangled tail –
Who splits the night with a woeful wail –
Past the dog who barks with fright
(Bow-wow-wow! in the Christmas night),
Past the goat who teeters there,
Entreating, bleating in despair,
To save the kitten who climbed so far
To cling with her claws to the Christmas star.
Branch to branch, and bough to bough,
The pigs will rescue the kitten now.

But what a disaster! Look at the pigs,
Their trotters totter among the twigs!
Help! Help! Arouse the town
Before the pigs come tumbling down.

Squealing! Bleating! Barking, too,
While the cat and the kitten moan and mew!
Carolling children stop to stare
At all the animals clinging there.
The children think it's a jamboree:
What an astonishing Christmas tree!

But as the animals huff and puff,
The kitten decides she's had enough.
Look! Look! She's begun to climb.
The kitten was tricking them all the time.

She ducks. She dives. As she descends
She steps in turn on all her friends.
Through piney needles and bending twigs
She lightly leaps on squealing pigs.
She purrs and pounces . . . seems to float,
Grabbing the beard of the bleating goat.
She runs along the back of the dog,
While all the children stand agog.
On to the cat, then down to the ground,
Landing happily – safe and sound.

But pigs and goat and dog and cat
Are stuck in the tree – and that is that!
Help! Help! I hear them call.
Catch us quickly in case we fall . . .

Goodness gracious, what do you see?
Someone is climbing the Christmas tree
To save the cat, and the dog as well,
(Oh, what a story they'll have to tell!)
Climbing the tree to get the goat
And brush the needles out of her coat –
Helping the pigs, both pink and brown,
To curl their tails as they scramble down.

Back once more on solid ground,
They frolic and rollick, safe and sound.
No more worry about a fall,
For somebody brave has saved them all
And taken them home for some Christmas fun,
With cakes and crackers for everyone.
Somebody brave has set them free.
Goodness gracious, can it be me?

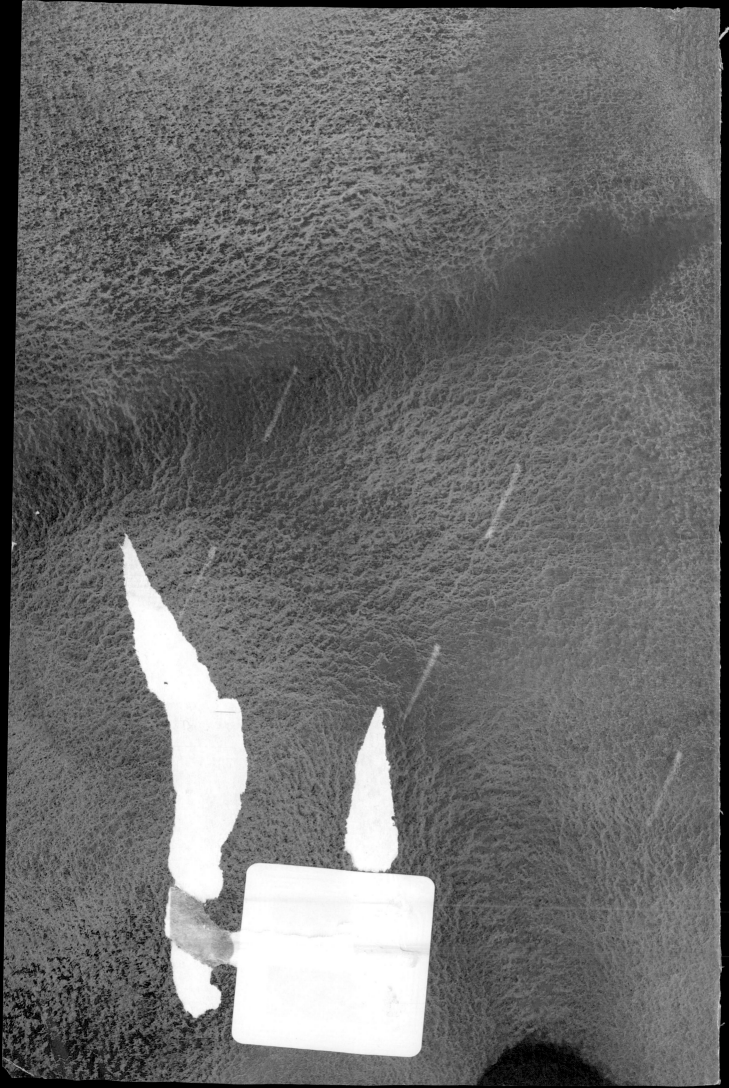